D1708303

LITTLE NASTY

by the same author

ff

LITTLE NASTY

Ruth Tomalin

faber and faber
LONDON · BOSTON

First published in 1985
by Faber and Faber Limited
3 Queen Square London WC1N 3AU

Filmset by Wilmaset
Birkenhead Merseyside
Printed in Great Britain by
Redwood Burn Limited
Trowbridge Wiltshire

British Library Cataloguing in Publication Data

Tomalin, Ruth
Little Nasty.
I. Title
823'.914[J]   PZ7

ISBN 0–571–13420–3

"The best revenge is to lead a happy life."

A SPANISH SAYING

1

Mother fell off the kitchen table while she was painting the ceiling, and that was the end of the best summer holidays Anna could remember.

Anna was out when it happened. She had run down to the shops to buy things for supper. And when she got back – Mother was lying there on the floor, looking very white and queer, with her friend Beth Pringle giving her sips of coffee from a spoon.

Anna had left the street door on the latch when she went out, and Mrs Pringle had called in to see Mother, and found her lying there. She had telephoned for an ambulance, and now Mother was going to hospital.

"The ambulance will be here in a minute," Mrs Pringle said. "And don't worry about Anna," she told Mother. "Of course she'll come to us, and Ming too. Don't worry about *anything*," she begged them, her kind face creased with her own worry.

Anna couldn't speak. She could only stand

there, clutching her parcels, too shocked to say a word. But when Mrs Pringle went downstairs to look out for the ambulance, she dropped quickly to the floor, whispering, "Oh Mother . . ."

Mother tried to smile, but even that seemed to hurt. "Oh Anna." She shut her eyes. "So silly of me. I can't think how – I just stepped back – and here I was."

"Oh *Mother*."

"It's just my back . . . hurts a bit. It's nothing really. I'll be home tomorrow, I expect."

"Yes," Anna whispered. "Yes."

Footsteps on the stairs and voices . . . Then Anna couldn't stop herself. She begged, "Oh, please. Please. Can't I stay here? Oh, do let me. Do tell her I can."

Mother gave a tiny shake of the head, and winced with pain. No use: Anna saw that. They wouldn't let her stay here alone.

Daddy was away; he'd been away all that year, working in Scotland. Gran had gone pony-trekking. She always did that in September. Mr and Mrs Mali, in the flat below, were away in India. There was no one else.

But, again, she couldn't help it. She whispered, "I don't want to go and stay with *them*. I – they – oh Mother," she almost sobbed.

Mother opened her eyes, and saw the look on Anna's face. She was astonished. "But – Robin and Linnet – we've known them so long! Ever

since play-group. Not like strangers – and Beth's
so kind . . ."

There was no time to say any more. The
ambulance men were in the room, covering
Mother with a blanket, lifting her gently on to
the stretcher, carrying her downstairs. The white
doors shut, the ambulance moved off. Gone.
Anna stared after it.

But Mrs Pringle led her quickly up to the flat,
talking all the time in quiet reassuring tones,
helping her to pack a suitcase, to find bags for
Ming's cat-litter and special food, then to lock up
safely.

"You can carry Ming, can't you? I'm sure he'll
like that better than a basket. So lucky I brought
the car. What a nice surprise for Robin and
Linnet!" (A nice surprise, ho ho, Anna thought.)
"Now, shall we go home and have tea? Then it'll

be time to ring the hospital and find out about Mother.''

No, it wasn't like going to stay with strangers. Strangers would have been all right.

Mrs Pringle was nice, yes. So was Mr Pringle. On rainy mornings, driving the twins to school, they would always call for Anna, to save her a wet walk. But they simply didn't *know*. And you couldn't tell them, or Mother either.

The play-group lady had known, and the teacher at the nursery school, and now the staff at King's Croft primary school. But fathers and mothers were different. You weren't supposed to tell tales. And those two were so clever – somehow there was never really anything to tell. Anna had never been able to breathe a word to Mother . . .

A word about what? Simply, that she and a lot of others at the play-group, and nursery school, and now at King's Croft, had learned to keep as far away as possible from Robin and Linnet Pringle.

2

Up till now, these had been wonderful holidays: mainly because of Ming.

He was Anna's cat. Her first pet. Even now, after she'd had him for six months, it still seemed a miracle that she'd been allowed to keep him.

No pets, Mr Mali the landlord had said, when they took the flat upstairs. You could see why: a cat or dog would have to be let out, and might spoil his beautiful garden, the pride of his life.

It was Ming himself who changed all that.

One day last spring Mother and Anna had passed a house with a notice on the gate – *Kittens free to good homes*. A brood of kittens played up and down the path inside the gate.

Anna clutched at Mother, exclaiming, "Oh, look!" One of the kittens broke away from the rest and came staggering to greet them. It was marked like a baby panda in broad pools of glossy black and white, like Indian ink on snow.

Anna cried, "Oh," and then – "Oh, *couldn't*

we?" And Mother said regretfully, "Darling, you know we can't. It's no good. Come away *now*."

As she spoke, the kitten rolled over on its back, wriggling and laughing up at them, saying as plainly as possible, "See how beautiful I am?" White furry face and stomach, black ears and eye patches, sparkling green eyes . . . They had never seen such an engaging and friendly little creature.

Mother laughed and said, "Ohhhhhh," and hesitated. Before she could speak again, Anna had the gate open, and she was clasping the purring kitten and talking very fast.

"We can get a litter-box, he needn't ever go in the garden. I'll take him to the park, every day, after school, so he can run about. Oh do say yes, oh do say yes, do!"

"It's not what *I* say, Anna. You know it's not. But we can't lose our flat. That's what it would mean. Anna, we have to be sensible –"

But the kitten was still in Anna's arms, rubbing its nose against her chin as though they had known each other for years. Its nose was pale pink, and cold, like a frosty spindleberry. Tiny claws, as sharp as pins, dug into her wrists. She said huskily,

"Can't we borrow him? Just for today? And – find out?"

"Well . . . but it's up to Mr Mali whether he stays. *You* must ask him. And if it's No – then that must be the end of it, and no fuss."

14

Anna promised. She'd have promised anything, just to have a kitten for one day, a kitten like this.

Mr Mali did say No, at once, and very firmly, when Anna went down that evening. He said it before Anna could speak, but with regret, because he was a kindly man.

She knew he meant it. She hadn't dared to hope for anything else, and yet the disappointment was so great that she couldn't begin to plead, to explain how careful she'd be not to let the kitten do any harm, if only, if only . . . Tears came into her eyes, and she was just going to turn away when the kitten gave a wild squirm and escaped from her hands, and jumped to the floor.

Then he rolled on his back, wriggling and showing off, just as he had done this morning: laughing up at Mr Mali, waiting for him to say "Ohhhhh" – as people always would, when he did that trick.

Anna heard Mr Mali draw in his breath. She waited, trembling, for him to say something cross. But what he did say, slowly, in grave and courteous tones, was –

"A fine cat. A very fine cat."

There was a long pause. Even the kitten seemed to feel it. He stopped wriggling, and glanced up as though in surprise, because no one was telling him yet how pretty he was. Anna broke the silence, faltering, "I wouldn't ever let him go in your garden, I promise . . ."

No good, she thought. But Mr Mali was still gazing down, watching the kitten. At last he spoke again.

"A cat likes to go out. He likes to wander and play. You must not keep him shut up all day."

"The park – " Anna began, and choked, because suddenly he was smiling: at the kitten, and at her too. He said,

"We will see. You may take him into the garden after school. I give permission. But you will not let him dig in the flower-beds? Very well, very well."

A miracle.

"It was *him*," Anna told Mother, dancing and laughing upstairs in the kitchen, squeezing the kitten till he squeaked. "He just knows everyone likes him, when he does that trick they can't help themselves. Oh you're such a show-off," she told the kitten, "aren't you? Aren't you?"

They named him Ming. He grew into a handsome young cat, still with his kittenish trick of rolling on his back to greet strangers. It never failed. They all said, "Ohhhhh!" and "Ahhhhh" and thought him charming. It even worked with people who didn't like cats at all: the bird-watching lady next door, Gran at the sea-side, owners of snappy little dogs in the park.

At school there was a picture of a cat with gold

earrings and a gold nose-ring. Anna thought Ming was that sort of cat. When Mother made him a collar, she sewed red and green jewels on it, saved from a Christmas cracker.

And he was tactful, as well as proud and charming. At first, when he and Anna played in Mr Mali's garden, Mrs Mali would be keeping a nervous eye on them from her window. But soon she was smiling at his antics, while he chased his feather mouse on the lawn, or played tigers in the flower-beds.

These were the most splendid Anna had ever seen, and she knew that each plant was special, loved and treasured by its owner. Tulips and irises in the spring; then lilies and marigolds, lush geraniums, petunias the colour of sugar almonds, pink and mauve and white. There were rose-trees on slender stems, and bowers of scented white jasmine and honeysuckle growing along the fence.

Ming would disappear into the undergrowth, moving like a feather cat, so lightly that the plants hardly stirred. Once he was out of sight, Anna could seldom find him. He would jump out at her from one end of the flower-bed while she was searching for him at the other end. Or he would run up a rose-tree, so quickly and delicately that no petal dropped, and jump to the top of the fence, and leap in a graceful curving dance like a dolphin's, all round the garden.

A tame hedgehog lived among the plants, coming out at dusk to eat bread-and-milk on the lawn. Mr Mali invited Ming to come down again after supper, and play with the hedgehog, because it amused him so much to see them together.

The hedgehog, Anna felt, was not amused. But Ming never harmed it, he would only paw at it gingerly, jumping away when he felt its bristles, then galloping round it with wild squeaks; while the hedgehog sucked up bread-and-milk and watched him all the time out of its bright shrewd little eyes.

When they came in from the garden, Anna would bury her nose in Ming's fur, that smelled of honey and pollen, marigold stalks and geranium leaves.

The summer holidays came, and Anna took him to the park every afternoon and let him race about and climb trees. This too was a great success: until one terrible day when Ming was chased by a greyhound, and ran away and couldn't be found for hours.

Anna searched and called, and so did two children whom she knew from school, Emily Something and her younger brother Jody. It was Emily who spotted him at last, when it was nearly nightfall and Anna nearly in despair.

He'd run up to the top of a tree and was clinging there, mewing plaintively, too frightened to come down. Anna, Emily and Jody all climbed up to rescue him; and next day Anna bought a round metal disc, a dog-tag, to go on his collar, with their telephone number on it, in case he ever got lost again.

Also, she tried to find Emily and Jody, to thank them again and ask them to tea.

This was Mother's idea. Sometimes she seemed worried because Anna didn't make friends at school. When they went for a picnic, or to a film, she would say, "Wouldn't you like to ask Robin and Linnet?" and Anna would say quickly, "No." Then Mother would look puzzled, and suggest someone else, and Anna would mutter, "I don't know them really. Not well enough."

She couldn't say, "I don't think they like me enough," but that was the truth. And that was why it was so lovely to have Ming, who had seemed to like her from the start.

She did try to find Emily and Jody, because

they'd been friendly as well as helpful. She thought she knew where they lived, but it turned out that they'd moved house a year before, and no one could tell her their new address, and they weren't in the park that day.

Next day, she and Mother and Ming went to stay at the sea with Gran; and at first Gran looked coldly at Ming, and murmured that she'd never cared for cats, they scratched the furniture and left fluff all over the place and gave her hay-fever.

But Ming kept his claws sheathed, and purred at her a good deal, not only at meal times, and at last performed his famous trick, rolling on his back and laughing up at her. And she actually smiled back, and began to say "Ohhhh" like everyone else, and then changed it to a kind of snort.

But within a day or two, Anna and Mother noticed, she was buying his favourite treats, scampi and blackberry yoghourt, and no more was heard of fluff or hay-fever.

Ming enjoyed the beach as he enjoyed everything else: racing about on the sand, scrambling over rocks, strutting on breakwaters, collecting new admirers.

They came back at the end of August – ready for the fray, as Mother said. The last part of the holidays was to be spent doing up the flat: stripping each room, shampooing carpets, washing curtains and covers, brushing down walls, then painting them in fresh soft colours, cream and apricot and primrose.

The Malis had gone off on their holiday; a friend of Mr Mali's came in each evening to water the garden, and he stayed to do some of the painting. Anna helped with everything, and rushed out to buy delicious picnic meals, ham rolls or curry, grapes and peaches, boxes of crisp fried chicken almost too hot to carry home.

Only Ming hated the whole upheaval, and kept out of the way between meals, dozing on Anna's bed.

He was there now, when Anna and Mrs Pringle came upstairs: stretching and mewing lazily, knowing nothing of what had happened, or what was going to happen. Nothing about poor Mother, or the move up to Foxhills Road to stay with the Pringles.

She could stick anything – even being in the same flat with those two – so long as Mother got well quickly. But what about Ming? Anna looked at him, and shivered suddenly.

3

Anna and Ming were given a little guest-room to themselves. That was a good thing, anyway. But Mrs Pringle said,

"You two, go and help Anna get unpacked before tea."

Linnet strolled in, and Robin followed, shutting the door. They sat side by side on the bed and watched her. Anna put Ming on the floor and he tiptoed about, inspecting the new place. Robin swung a foot at him and asked Linnet,

"What's *that* supposed to be?"

Linnet shrugged. "She calls it *Mingy*. Or is it Mangy?"

Anna told herself – Whatever they say – I've got to keep quiet. It's the only way.

Ming saw the pair watching him. He ran up and rolled on his back, boxing at them with his paws. The trick had never failed yet.

It failed now.

They looked at him coldly. Linnet said, "What a ragbag." Robin said, "Ugh."

Ming wriggled and purred a moment longer, then stopped and twisted his head round to see what could be the matter. He was puzzled. By now, they should have been saying, "Ohhh" and trying to stroke him, while he pretended to bite them.

Suddenly he sat up, turned his back and began very carefully to lick at a tangle in his fur. Anna knew his feelings were hurt, and she burned with anger. Still she ignored them and went on unpacking. There was sand in the suitcase, from that lovely time at the sea, only ten days ago . . .

Each time she took out a shirt, or a sweater, or a pair of sports shoes, Robin and Linnet would glance at each other and grin, or raise their eyebrows. Anna couldn't help wondering – was there really something wrong with her things? – even though she knew there wasn't. She unrolled her swim-suit, and Robin said,

"Will she come swimming with *us*? In *that*?"

Linnet shrugged again, and giggled. Anna quickly took out a book she'd brought, and put it on the bedside table. Linnet reached across for the book, opened it and read from inside the cover, " 'Happy birthday Anastasia'. Well, well. So that's her real name, is it?"

She'd forgotten Mother had written that. If only she'd chosen something else . . . she said quickly, "Of course it's not!"

"Oh. Whose book is this, then?"

"Mine . . ."

"Well then. 'Love from Mother.' There you are. *She* wouldn't get your name wrong."

"Let's look," Robin drawled. "An-as-tas-ia. *An ass stays here*. Well, that's true, anyway."

Linnet shrieked with laughter. Anna said, her voice trembling in spite of herself,

"It's just a nickname." And it's private, she thought.

"Nasty for short, I suppose," said Robin.

"Yes. Little Nasty. Suits her, doesn't it?"

"Mm. No one likes her, do they?"

"Shouldn't think so. Tell us, Anastasia. Who likes you?"

She was silent.

"There, you see. She can't think of anyone."

She said defiantly, "Yes, I can . . ."

"Go on. Who?"

"My father and mother. And my Gran."

"They don't count. They have to put up with you."

"And Ming does."

"Cats aren't people. Try again."

Ming *is* a person. She didn't say this aloud. She rushed on, her temper rising,

"Mrs Grace at school."

"I have news for you," Robin said grandly. "She thinks you're a horrid little thing. As a matter of fact."

"She doesn't like *you*!" Anna blazed. "I heard her say to Miss Eliot – 'Not Angels but Pringles!' She meant *you*! When you spoilt the Christmas play – it was you let the hamsters loose, and you knew the Virgin Mary was scared of them – "

As the angry words rushed out, she realized that the two faces looking at her had taken on a different expression. They lost their sharp look and became bland and innocent. Anna stopped in dismay. Too late, she saw that the door had opened and their mother was standing there.

She must have heard what I said, Anna thought miserably. How awful. Like telling tales.

But Mrs Pringle only said in her gentle voice,

"Are you looking after Anna? Come along now. Ming too, Anna. That's right."

As they sat down at the kitchen table, Linnet whispered,

"Cheer up, Little Nasty. They could have named you Anna Maria. Like that rat in *Samuel Whiskers*."

"Or Anaconda," Robin added. "A kind of snake," he said aloud, as his mother brought the hot plates from the stove. "Mum, can't we take Anna to a zoo?"

"What a good idea," she agreed. Robin and Linnet smirked.

When Anna had been small she'd had a secret name for Mrs Pringle: Mrs Brown. Not only was she brown herself, in different shades – hair, eyes and complexion, long summer caftans and beads – but the food she gave you was mostly brown too. Like this tea: beans on toast, brown bread, dates, dark honey, chocolate biscuits. As a rule Anna liked all these things, and so did Ming. Now she could hardly swallow a mouthful, and he sat on her knee, refusing everything . . . almost as though he were sulking. But Ming *never* sulked.

Linnet stroked him, then noticed the disc on his collar and read out the telephone number.

"Whatever's that for?"

"So his friends can ring him up," said Robin.

"Oh, very witty. I was asking *you*, Anna."

With Mrs Pringle there, she had to answer. She mumbled,

"Just – in case he got lost."

"No use now, though," Robin pointed out. "No one in your flat to answer."

"Oh well," their mother said, "it's not going to happen! We'll take great care of him, won't we, Anna?"

"Yes," Linnet said thoughtfully. "We must see he doesn't get lost."

4

The news from the hospital was partly good and partly bad. Mother hadn't broken any bones; but they wouldn't let her come home right away. She had to stay there for a bit and rest – "just to make sure," the doctor said.

Anna had a fresh gleam of hope when the phone rang later that evening, and it was Daddy, calling from Scotland. She thought – "He's flying down tonight! We can go home!" But, standing there while he and Mrs Pringle talked, she realized that that wouldn't happen yet.

Daddy had spoken to the doctor too, and to Mother. She was in bed now, feeling better already, she'd said. And the plan was that Daddy should take leave from his work and come home to look after her when she left hospital – *if* the Pringles could *very* kindly keep Anna till then?

Mrs Pringle cried, "Now don't say a word about that! We all love having her!" Anna's heart sank.

Then Daddy spoke to *her*, saying what a shame it all was, but Mother would soon be well, and he'd see them both in just a few days.

A few days . . . it didn't sound long. But, looking back, Anna would feel that those were the longest days she'd ever lived through.

It was all right, more or less, when Mrs Pringle was there; and she was there most of the time. But each afternoon she went to visit Mother, and Anna couldn't go with her, as no one under twelve was allowed in. She came to dread those afternoon hours, not for herself so much as for Ming.

Not that the twins were openly cruel to him. At least, they didn't pull his tail or kick him. But in the kitchen they would flick drops of water at him; and in the play-room they would drop things or make a sudden loud noise to startle him. He was losing his proud ways and glossy looks, and growing thin and jumpy.

They were in the play-room most afternoons, as it was raining. With anyone else, Anna would have found this interesting. Robin had spent a good deal of the holidays making a huge model of a spacecraft, in balsa wood and plastic and silver foil. It stood on a launching pad, with the tiny crew all ready to get in, wearing white space-suits covered with straps and tubes and packs, and great boots and gloves, and helmets with plastic visors.

At another table, Linnet was doing a giant jigsaw. This too was well on the way to being finished. The picture on the box showed four children grandly dressed in old-fashioned clothes, one of them a boy with a musical box. Behind this pretty smiling group there was something else, not pretty at all: a wicked-looking cat. It had jumped on a chair-back, and hung there goggling at a frightened bird in a cage.

Linnet was busy with the girls' dresses: stiff bodices, flounces, billowing skirts. She told Anna, "You can do that cat if you like – " for a moment her face had a cat-like gleam – "as you're so keen on cats."

"Ming isn't like that!"

"Not *nasty*? Never goes after birds?" Fitting in a frilled sleeve, Linnet added,

"If he ever got lost, he'd have to learn."

She'd said something like that before . . . Anna asked sharply,

"What do you mean?"

"To catch birds or mice. Or he might starve."

"He isn't going to get lost!" (And we said that before, too, she thought uneasily.)

"Of course not," Linnet agreed, hunting for another piece.

Ming had been sitting on the window-seat. Suddenly he shot to the floor, spitting angrily. At the same moment Robin gave a cry: somehow, an open bottle of gum had slipped from his hand and spilled itself over Ming.

"Oh, bother that animal! Why does it have to be so clumsy? Yuck," he added, grinning, "now it's all sticky!"

Anna snatched Ming up. "He isn't clumsy! It was you – *you* – " She fled to the bathroom, locked herself in, sponged Ming with warm water and dried him carefully. But the stickiness and the sharp sweetish smell of gum still clung to him. When she carried him to their own room, he hid under the bed, huddled in a cross bundle, ears flattened. When Anna tried gently to pull him out, he snapped and growled. She was appalled. He'd never done such a thing before.

What was she to do? Tell their mother? But Robin would only say, "Mum, it was an accident," and she would believe him. How could she help it? So what was Anna to do?

Mother rang every evening from a bedside telephone. Anna was left alone in the hall, with the telephone and the ticking clock, to talk to her. Mother always said she was feeling much better, and she'd be home before long, and she hoped Anna and Ming were enjoying themselves. Anna could only say Yes, and please come home soon. Suppose she were to say, "They're tormenting Ming"?

That evening she did almost say it. But not quite. It might make Mother feel worse, then

31

she'd have to stay in longer perhaps . . . The clock whirred and began to chime, and she put down the phone and went slowly back to the play-room.

Linnet said softly, "Having a *lovely* time, she says."

"So glad."

"Isn't her mother coming out *yet*?"

"Oh, we're stuck with her for ages, I expect."

"Seems ages now. Can't she go somewhere else?"

"What, Little Nasty? and that gruesome animal? No one else would have them."

The morning after the gum spill, Mrs Pringle herself was having a long talk on the telephone. Linnet and Anna were in the kitchen, washing up, while Robin hoovered up and down the passage. Ming had gone to hide under the bed again, and Anna left him there: it seemed the safest place.

Suddenly she heard a dreadful sound. The Hoover seemed to go wild, not buzzing steadily but roaring and howling. Above the din came a shout from Robin, then a terrible shriek. Ming's voice.

As Anna dashed for the door, Ming came hurtling into the kitchen, his fur on end, his eyes crossed. Claws scrabbling madly, he leapt on to the table. A bottle of milk went crashing, eggs smashed and dripped, a bag of flour burst over the floor.

32

Mrs Pringle came running in. She found Robin laughing, while Anna faced him. Ming struggled in her arms, tearing and scratching, but she didn't feel any of that. She screamed at Robin,

"You *chased* him with the Hoover! You did! You did!" Tears poured down her face. She rushed into her bedroom and banged the door.

Outside, she could hear just what she expected.

"Mum, honestly, I didn't do anything. Ming ran out, and he got in the way, but I dodged him. You heard me pulling the Hoover back! It never touched him, he's only scared a bit, of course – "

And then Linnet: "Yes, I saw. It wasn't Robin's fault."

And Mrs Pringle, speaking for a long time, very quietly:

"Upset about her mother . . . must be specially nice . . . we'll think of something . . . take her mind off . . . all right, Robin . . ."

Yes, they got away with everything. They'd been doing it as long as Anna could remember.

5

Then came a day Anna would never forget.

The morning was all right. They played rounders with some older boys and girls on the grass behind the flats. Ming was left safely upstairs on Anna's bed.

But after dinner it rained again. As she left for the hospital, Mrs Pringle said as usual, "All right, Anna?" And then to Linnet,

"What are you going to do?"

"Jigsaw," Linnet said. "We'll finish it today."

Robin was already in the play-room working at his model, with the radio playing.

It was the first time Anna had been alone with them, since the Hoover affair. Yesterday afternoon, Mrs Pringle had driven them into the country to a wildlife park, where there were deer and badgers and foxes. Now Anna decided to escape to her own room and paint pictures of these animals to send to Mother.

But Linnet followed her, and began to make a fuss of Ming, playing with his feather mouse and trying to make him run after it. Then she said,

"Anna, don't you think he's hungry? He didn't eat much dinner, you know. I think he'd like some more."

Without waiting for Anna to agree, she picked him up and carried him into the kitchen, and filled his dish with cold macaroni cheese. Ming turned away in scorn; but when Linnet opened the fridge and took out a carton of yoghurt, he changed his mind, and after a certain amount of coaxing he actually settled down to eat.

Anna stayed with him. Linnet strolled away into the sitting-room and gazed out of the front window. Suddenly she called –

"Anna! Look! Here's the hospital van – the one they take people home in. Do come and see – oh, oh, it's stopping here – quick! Suppose they've sent your mother home today!"

Anna raced to join her at the window.

She couldn't see the van. "Parked behind the hedge," Linnet called. She was at the door already. Anna caught her up, and they rushed downstairs together, and across the forecourt to the hedge. But there was no van. Nothing parked there at all.

"That's queer," Linnet said. "I *did* see it stop here, Anna. Must have driven off again. How funny."

Anna didn't think it was funny. Another of Linnet's jokes, a specially nasty one . . . She stalked upstairs again without a word.

In the kitchen, Ming's dish had tipped over, spilling a mess of yoghurt. He wasn't there. Anna ran to their room and looked under the bed. Next moment she was back in the kitchen. Linnet was sponging up the mess, but Anna had a quick glimpse of her face, bent over this task. She was smiling.

"Where is he? *Where is he?*"

Linnet looked up. No smile now, only blank surprise.

Anna stared at her, then raced to look in the other rooms. He wasn't anywhere. She opened the play-room door crying "Ming! Ming!" Robin was tilting his chair in front of the cupboard, working hard at his model, with the radio on at full blast. He shouted, "What's up?"

Behind her, Linnet shrieked, "The front door – Anna, Anna! He must've followed us down – quick, Anna – "

They ran into the road. Linnet gasped, "You go that way, I'll take this – he can't have gone far!"

The rain had stopped, but the trees dripped and the pavement shone with wetness. Anna *knew* that Ming wouldn't have left the front steps – he could never bear to get his paws wet. He wouldn't even cross Mr Mali's lawn on a wet day. Then a thought struck her. A dog – he might have been frightened by a dog – like that greyhound in the park! She ran down Foxhills Road calling "Ming, Ming," looking in front gardens, stopping passers-by to gasp, "Please, have you seen a cat? Black and white – with a jewelled collar?" No one had seen him.

At last she turned and retraced her steps, cold panic clutching her now, making her feel dull and slow, the way you felt in a nightmare. But Linnet might have found him! Or – another flash of hope – he might have dashed up a tree, just as he'd done that day in the park . . . She moved blindly, gazing up into one tree after another, still calling – until she almost ran straight into Linnet.

"Oh – Linnet – have you – "

Linnet broke in excitedly, "Look, if someone finds him, they'll ring your number, won't they? The one on his collar?"

Anna's face lit up. Of course! He wouldn't be lost for long. Someone was sure to find him, and then – "Oh, yes, yes, of course they'll ring! I'll go there and wait, I'll go *now*!"

She was darting away when Linnet caught her wrist.

"Anna, you're *stupid*, aren't you? How can you get in, you haven't got the keys – you know they're in Mum's handbag!"

Anna tore her hand away. "I'll get in," she

said grimly, and would have set off down the road again. But Linnet grabbed her hand, gabbling,

"This way! This way! There's a short cut – you'll be there in half the time . . ."

Anna fought her, gasping, "Leave me alone. It's all your fault. Oh, Ming, oh Ming – "

"Well, you want to get there, don't you? The quickest way? Someone could be ringing *now*, he might be found already!"

"Oh yes – oh yes – he might be. Go on, go on – " They set out at top speed for Anna's home, running hand in hand, like friends.

6

Linnet led her round to the back of the flats, over the grass, through a hedge, into a wild part of the garden. They dodged among shrubs and brambles, slipping and sliding on the soaking turf, skirting a nettle patch. Then they were scrambling over a fence, dropping into a narrow lane, racing on and on . . . They came to an old railway track, crossed it by an arching bridge – and they were in an alley between high fences, and suddenly Anna knew where she was. The alley came out into a road, and there ahead was her own home . . .

She darted across the road, ahead of Linnet now – crashed through the front gate, ran round to the side of the house, and then stopped, looking up . . . all the windows were shut, of course. But there was the rose trellis that went up by Mr Mali's porch. From there she could scramble up the drainpipe somehow, somehow, to their own bathroom window sill – and break the window, and get inside. She *knew* she could do it. She must . . . and then it would be all right. She only had to wait by the telephone, until someone found Ming, and rang to tell her.

At any other time she would have been afraid of this perilous climb; but not now. She even remembered to grab a stone from the rockery and stuff it into her pocket, ready to break the glass. She was already half-way up the trellis when Linnet caught her ankle, shrieking,

"Wait – I forgot! I've got the keys after all – look, they're here – we can get in – "

Anna dropped down and stared at the latch-keys that Linnet was dangling in front of her . . . The nightmare feeling came back. Linnet must have taken those keys from her mother's bag – before her mother went out. *Before Ming was lost . . .*

She had been scarlet from running. Now she turned white. She stared from the keys to Linnet's face, and began to tremble, without quite knowing why. Before she could speak Linnet turned away, with a little toss of her head, and ran to unlock the street door.

Anna was behind her as she pushed it open. And then they both heard a sound from the flat upstairs: a faint continuous brrr-brrr. *The phone was ringing.*

She snatched the keys from Linnet, took the stairs in three jumps, and a moment later she was gasping into the receiver,

"Yes, oh yes, it's me. Have you found him? Where are you?"

But no one answered. And yet they hadn't rung off, she was sure. Anna gave her number and asked again, "Please, have you found my cat? A black and white cat with – oh," she almost shrieked, "don't go, don't . . ."

But the caller was gone already. The phone had clicked: the line was dead. And – he hadn't been quite quick enough. For, as she was speaking, Anna had caught a sound at the other end. Something she knew quite well. The first soft chime of the clock in the Pringles' hall, beginning to strike four.

Anna knew now. She saw it all. And she swung round with such a look on her face that Linnet felt almost afraid.

"*You*," Anna said slowly. "It was you and *him* . . ."

Linnet tried to carry it off. "What do you mean, Anna? Who was it ringing? Have they found Ming?"

Anna took two steps and got her by the shoulders. "Stop that," she said sternly. "Do you hear? – No, he's not found. He was never lost. Oh, *what have you done with him*?"

But she didn't wait for an answer. She shook Linnet hard, and pushed her away, brushed past and rushed down the stairs.

She was running again, faster than ever, away

up to Foxhills Road. And, as she ran, she suddenly began to remember . . . the play-room, with the radio blaring, and Robin's chair tilting against the door of the cupboard.

So that was it. While Linnet got her out of the way, Robin had snatched him out of the kitchen, and locked him in the cupboard, with that pop music drowning his cries. Was he in there still? But he might be dead – how could he breathe, in a place like that, a Black Hole, with a cruel jailer keeping the door shut tight?

Yes, he must be dead, he must be . . . But Anna prayed as she ran – Please don't let him die. Let me get there in time.

She reached the Pringles' flat, and put her finger on the bell and held it there.

Mrs Pringle opened the door. She was still in her coat, just back. "Anna," she said in surprise. "You?" And then – "Anna! What is it? What's happened?"

Anna didn't answer. She rushed blindly into the hall, and stopped dead.

Ming was sitting there, by the hall clock, washing himself. Washing, and sneezing. He looked huffy and ruffled, but he was alive, unhurt. Anna picked him up and buried her face in his fur.

It had a sharp sweetish smell. The smell of gum. So she'd been right: the play-room cupboard reeked of gum, and paint, and all the

stuff Robin used to put his model together. Now Ming was reeking of it too. He struggled to get down, and go on with his washing. Poor Ming. Snatched away from his dish, bundled into the smelly dark, choking and sneezing – and she'd let it all happen. No wonder he was fed up with everyone for the moment.

Linnet came in one way, and Robin the other, and they stood together, watching her: each with a small grin of triumph. Oh yes, the plot had worked all right. Even better than they could have dreamed. She'd fallen right into the trap.

Mrs Pringle said again, "Anna. Something's the matter – "

Robin broke in, "Hullo, Mum. Come and see what I've been doing – "

44

"Wait. Anna – "

Linnet said impatiently, "It's all right, really. We couldn't find Ming, we thought he'd run out, but you see he was here all the time, Anna! No need to get excited."

"He was shut in. I looked everywhere – " She stopped, feeling almost frantic, because she knew it was no good trying to tell what had happened. Even if she could find the words, it would all be a waste of time, their mother would never believe her.

"Didn't look hard enough, did you?" Robin grinned. And then,

"Mum, you know she gets in a state. All about *nothing* . . ."

All about nothing. It was too much. Anna couldn't speak, she was shivering too hard. Hatred seemed to choke her; a great sob gathered in her throat.

She looked wildly round the hall, at the clock that had given Robin away, the telephone he'd used to torment her. Then she did the worst thing she could think of. She took two steps to the table, picked up the whole telephone set in both hands, and slung it with all her strength at those two mocking faces.

7

An owl shrieked in a tree next morning, and Anna woke with a jump.

It was very early, with faint grey light in the room, and mist hiding the trees outside. Ming was curled beside her, and she put out a finger to stroke his ears. This had always been the signal for him to wriggle and purr; but now he stayed glumly asleep.

Anna remembered something she'd heard at school, about dolphins. Dolphins were the most friendly and good-tempered creatures in the world. But even a dolphin, if it were teased and provoked in a nasty manner, could lose its playful trusting ways and turn nasty too, and even learn to snap. That had happened to Ming.

As for herself – she remembered, with deep shame, the awful thing she'd done with that telephone. Not that she'd really done any harm, as it turned out. Robin and Linnet had dodged out of the way, and the telephone had crashed on to the rug, with a fearful din but no damage. It was still working when Robin picked it up.

Mother had rung as usual in the evening, and Mrs Pringle had talked to her for some time before calling Anna. When she was left alone in the hall, Anna asked Mother, "Did – did Mrs Pringle tell you something – about me?"

And Mother said, "She thought you'd been rather upset. Ming went missing, didn't he? – but I'm so glad he was all right . . . darling, I'll be out very soon now, I promise. It's school next week, isn't it? We'll have to do some quick shopping, won't we? – new everything, I expect – "

They talked about that, and Anna had felt almost cheerful by the time they rang off. But now she felt as glum as Ming.

School . . . she wasn't looking forward to the new term any more. *They* said Mrs Grace thought her horrid. Suppose that was true? Suppose everything they said about her was true, after all?

Mrs Pringle had been kinder than ever all the evening, treating Anna as though she were ill, taking her temperature and bringing her a special hot drink when she was in bed. But, Anna thought – *she* must think I'm horrid too. Flying into tantrums. Linnet had whispered, "My mother's *surprised* at you," and Anna knew that, for once, she was telling the truth.

Also, she knew the sort of thing they would have said to their mother in private: "Oh, she's always doing things like that. No one likes her at school. As a matter of fact, they call her Little Nasty . . ."

And it was all so unfair!

That hateful plot yesterday – they shouldn't be allowed to get away with it. Somebody ought to pay them out.

It was then that a plot of her own darted into Anna's head. A revenge. It started just as an idea – "I wish something would happen to them. Something they'd really mind, like – like – " and suddenly it wasn't only a wish, it was a plan. She sat up in bed, tense and excited, knotting her hands into fists and beating them softly on the quilt as she thought it out.

Ming woke and stared at her, and she whispered aloud, "Ming – yes! Yes! That's what I'll do – it'll look just like an accident!"

Could she do it now, right away? Would there be time? She knew Mr Pringle always got up at six.

She crept to the door and listened. No bath water running or teacups tinkling. No sound at all. She tiptoed along to the hall clock. Only ten past five! Nearly an hour. Plenty of time . . . She slid back to her room, pulled on her slippers, lifted Ming and stole out, into the play-room, shutting the door behind her.

There was the beautiful jigsaw on the table, finished now. And Robin's wonderful model. She took a long look at both. A last look: in a few minutes, now, they'd be gone for ever.

She meant to take them quietly to bits, and leave the bits scattered all over the tables and the floor – as Ming had scattered the kitchen things, when Robin drove him mad with the Hoover. Then she'd leave Ming shut in here, and go back to bed and pretend to be asleep until everyone else was up. And then they'd find the wreckage.

Mr and Mrs Pringle would think Ming had been shut in quite by chance, and had got in a panic and done all the damage. But – and this was the best part – the twins would know the truth, and there would be nothing they could do about it. They couldn't say, "Anna did it on purpose". Their parents would be shocked at the idea – however horrid they thought her, they just wouldn't want to believe *that*.

It would be Robin's and Linnet's turn to feel helpless, and Anna's turn to look smug. Oh yes, a grand revenge. They'd named her Nasty, and that was what she was going to be.

And she'd take good care they didn't get another chance to harm Ming. Poor Ming . . . that was the bad part. He'd get the blame. And, besides, he wouldn't like being left in here. It wouldn't be as bad as being shut in that cupboard, but he'd be lonely. He'd think she had let him down again. Even now, crouching on the floor, he gave her such a cold look that she could hardly bear it.

"Only for a little while," she whispered. "Look, I'll find you something to eat first. Something nice. Then you won't really mind, will you?"

She hugged him, while he turned away his head, and then she carried him along to the kitchen.

There was a packet of the muesli he liked for breakfast, with the top of the milk. She spooned a reckless helping into his dish, and went to the fridge. Just as she lifted out the milk bottle, a small sound made her jump so that she almost dropped it. She looked round quickly – but it was all right. No one had come in.

The sound came again. From Ming. He'd come to life, and jumped on to the window-sill. All his gloom had vanished. He was gazing at something on the grass plot below. And – Anna realized – he looked exactly like the cat in the jigsaw picture, all ears and claws and fierce goggling eyes. A hunting cat.

She rushed to the window, just in time to see something bundle over the grass and disappear into the bottom of the hedge. A small animal, whitish. A squirrel? A rabbit? But it didn't hop like a rabbit or dance along like a squirrel. Could it be a hedgehog, like the one in Mr Mali's garden – only *white*? They must be pretty rare, she thought. And would it have ruby eyes, like an albino rabbit?

Ming was prancing on his hind legs, waving his paws and making dabs at the glass, as though he'd like to dive right through, and away, away after it – whatever it was. He whickered softly, and switched his tail, then ran to the door and looked back at Anna with a hard commanding stare.

This wasn't like Ming, with his kittenish tricks and his endearing ways . . . he'd never looked like that before! Eager, wicked, hungry – but not for milk or muesli.

A great wave of excitement came from him, and she felt herself caught up in his mood. She unlocked the outer door and followed him through it, down the back stairs and out into the misty light.

8

Anna had always thought, and said, "Ming can't bear to get his paws wet." But now he skipped across the dewy grass and through a gap in the hedge, so fast that she could hardly keep up with him. How clever, she thought – I believe he's following a scent, like a hound in a fox-chase. I never knew *he* could do that! There seemed, all of a sudden, a good deal she hadn't known about Ming.

Now they were in the wild part of the garden; but still Ming didn't hesitate. He jumped through the long rough grass with his curving dolphin swoops, and dived through spider-webs and gossamers that hung everywhere in shivering curtains, each thread outlined in drops of dew like bright pinheads.

Soon his coat was grey with gossamer strands, his paws and underside soaked with dew: and he didn't seem to care. He ran to and fro among the bushes – and then Anna caught a flash of white deep in the grass under a clump of

brambles. Ming had seen it too. With a whicker of excitement he plunged into the undergrowth.

Anna tried to go after him, but the thorns pierced her slippers, and brambles clung to her, holding her fast. She called, "Ming, Ming, come back," and peered into the bush, afraid she might never see him again.

In his wild mood, she hardly thought he would answer her call. But a moment later he *was* back, crouching against her legs, almost as though he were hiding. Yet he wasn't scared. His green eyes blazed, and he too stared into the depths of the bushes, giving little mews and twitches. Then he was gone again.

Trying to keep him in sight, Anna bent down and gazed after him. She saw that the undergrowth was honeycombed with little paths and tunnels. Ming was weaving his way in and out, following a trail. And – she realized – the air was heavy with a musky scent, as though a wild animal had its den nearby.

But what kind of animal? Hedgehogs didn't smell like that, or squirrels, so far as she knew; and rabbits smelt quite differently – hutch rabbits, anyway, like the ones in the pet shop where she bought Ming's litter.

Could there be a badger's sett in there? Or – marvellous thought – a fox's den?

Parting the thorny strands, trying to make her way further into the clump, she had another thought. A fox or a badger would be quite big. It might be big enough, and fierce enough, to kill a cat. And there was silly innocent Ming, chasing after it, with never a thought of danger . . .

Something black and white moved in there – a badger, yes! She stood up, ready to crash in somehow to the rescue. But it was Ming himself, skipping back along the tunnel, not frightened at all, but bold and amused. He rubbed quickly round her legs – at least he was friends with her again! – and then turned and dashed up a tree.

But not far. Quickly he backed down and came to sit by her for a moment, licking his paws.

It was lovely here, Anna thought. The mist shut them into a strange still world, like being in the middle of a forest, miles and miles from anywhere. Looking at the beautiful silvery webs that hung all around, she saw that in each one there was a large spider, pale brown and plump, like a sultana.

She drew a deep breath; and again she caught that strong musky smell. It *must* be from a fox? She couldn't remember if the ones in the wildlife park smelt like this; but everyone knew wild foxes had a strong scent. If only she could see it . . .

Again she found herself shivering with excitement. With cold, too. Her slippers were squelching, her wet pyjama legs clung to her ankles. Then Ming sneezed five times. Of course he was sopping . . . She must take him in and dry him. But she didn't want to go back, she wanted to stay here, hidden away from that other world, and go on watching for a fox.

Behind her came a tiny rustle in the grass. Almost before she'd heard it, Ming sprang away from her side, straight into the place from which the rustle came. And, as he came prancing back, he gave a cry she'd never heard before: a hunter's song of triumph.

He was carrying a mouse: a small brown thing with a long tail, drooping limply from his jaws. He dropped it at her feet, and again he gave that loud melodious howl. His first mouse – and of course it was clever of him; but Anna, stooping to touch the tiny damp corpse, wished it needn't have been so furry and pathetic, like a baby hamster.

She couldn't see any teeth marks on it; perhaps it had died of sheer fright. Ming sniffed at it doubtfully, and touched it with his paw . . . and then a queer thing happened.

The corpse opened large dark eyes and gazed up at Ming. And, instead of rushing away to safety, it sat up on its hind legs, and went on staring at him, its brilliant eyes agog, ears and whiskers quivering – not with fear, but with surprise and curiosity. If Ming was an innocent beginner, so was his prey.

He stared too, and backed away a few steps; and Anna seized her chance. She snatched up the mouse and tossed it into the middle of a nettle patch, and heard it scurry away. Ming darted after it, then checked himself, and began to run in circles, giving a low whimper of disappointment.

Anna laughed, and swept him up, whispering,

"Oh Ming, you don't want to eat *that*, you want muesli and lovely yog, and so you shall."

She took one quick look about her, thinking – we can come back here by ourselves. I'll get away somehow. I won't let them know where we are. A place of our own . . . She ran back towards the flats.

She had forgotten all about the grand revenge.

9

Everything seemed quite changed, now she had somewhere to escape to. Strange what a difference that made.

Robin and Linnet were just the same, with their usual sly whispers – "How's Little Nasty today then?" "What a wicked temper, dear, dear" – but she found she didn't care what they said. She wasn't even listening. Let them babble away . . . oh yes, and let them keep their jigsaw and spacecraft! They'd never know what had nearly happened to those . . .

She smiled to herself, remembering.

She didn't want to smash their things now. She only wanted to slip away, and get back to the wild garden as fast as possible.

And it was quite easy after all. This morning, those two were going to the dentist with their mother. Anna had only to ask, "May I stay here with Ming?" – and then, "Could we go out on the grass at the back?" It seemed a natural thing to ask. No one suspected anything. She took

Ming's feather mouse, and a tennis ball and racquet.

Last night, if she'd heard about the dentist, Anna would have thought nastily, I wish he'd jolly well pull out all your teeth, one by one, with no gas or dope or anything, and serve you right. Even though she knew it couldn't happen, the thought would have been a pleasure. Now she didn't bother wishing anything of the kind, she only wanted them out of the way.

When they were gone, she looked up warily at the other flats. No one was looking down from a balcony, or watching at a window. She took Ming and slipped through the hedge, and didn't stop running until she came to the brambles.

At least – she thought this must be the same place. Here was the tree Ming had climbed, the tuft of grass where he'd caught the mouse, the nettle patch where it escaped. And the musky animal smell was stronger now. But the mist had disappeared, and with it the grey mysterious forest where they'd been at dawn.

At first she felt a pang of disappointment. But soon, looking about, she could see that, even in broad daylight, this was a magical place. A wilderness: she'd always liked that word. And it was still theirs, with no one else in sight.

The sun shone warmly now, and dewdrops sparkled everywhere. So did the jewels on Ming's collar. Midges were dancing in little

clouds, and a robin fluttered about, scooping
them up. Spider-webs hung on the bushes,
blowing and drying in the breeze. One held a
captive fly, struggling and buzzing, while the
spider sat and watched: like a cat with a poor
mouse, Anna thought. She'd never expected to
feel sorry for a fly.

A soft chattering made her look up. Over the
fence, in the next garden, there was a high tree
with a few red apples. A squirrel had climbed to
the highest twig and was trying to get at an apple
that grew lower down, just out of reach. The

squirrel hung down by its tail and hind claws, the top hairs of its grey fur floating like gossamers, so that a line of silver light seemed to shimmer round it. Still it couldn't quite touch the apple. All the time it kept up a peevish sound like someone muttering, "Oh come here – you – you – *you* . . ." It teetered and swung – nearly there – and then, as it made a grab, the apple was gone.

In a flash of black and white, a magpie had swooped down, knocked the prize to the ground and dived after it. Anna heard a long mocking chuckle. The squirrel swung upright, gibbering with rage, jerking its tail and all but shaking its fist. Then it started to climb after another apple.

Ming had been watching wide-eyed. Now, before Anna could stop him, he was over the fence and up the tree, after the squirrel. In a moment they were lost to sight among the leaves; she could hear a thrashing of branches and a hissing noise.

Could Ming really catch a squirrel? She could hardly believe that was happening. Only this morning he'd been a beginner. What a hunter he was, and she'd never guessed!

The two came in sight again, and things were not quite like that. The squirrel was chasing Ming. Then Anna's bold hunter was back over the fence, and she was holding him safely. The squirrel darted up the tree again, and peered at them round the trunk, still muttering furiously.

Ming seemed quite unnerved. She thought he'd started that chase in fun: but the squirrel was in no mood for playing about.

To cheer Ming up, she carried him away to the far side of the brambles. They sat in the sun eating blackberries. There were different bushes here, green and low-growing, with small pink flowers and round white berries like peppermint balls. They formed a deep cave, a perfect hiding-place. She tucked Ming under her arm and crawled in.

They had been sitting for a few minutes in this cool leafy refuge when she saw something out there, under the brambles. Not a squirrel or a fox or a badger. It was the small animal she'd seen that morning: the white hedgehog!

She felt Ming stiffen on her knee. As they gazed, it moved into the open – and another after it.

Anna had dropped some blackberries on the grass. They ran across and nibbled them, cocking their ears and listening as though they sensed the watchers in the cave. And now Anna gave a gasp of surprise and delight. She knew what they were. Not hedgehogs. Wild guinea-pigs . . .

There seemed to be a large family, father and mother and two broods of young ones, some nearly full-grown, others not as big as tennis balls. All had spiky snow-white fur, bright dark eyes, snub-nosed faces, squeaky voices like Anna's old teddy-bear before he lost his voice.

They would come out from under the brambles in ones and twos, dodge back again and poke out from another tunnel, so that she couldn't be sure how many there really were.

Ming caused a panic when he first appeared, dancing out of the cave – not to hunt them, Anna knew, but to play. Squeaking in alarm, they dashed for cover; and he lay down, mewing softly, calling to them to come back. Word seemed to go round that he was harmless.

Soon Anna joined him in the open; and, before the morning ended, she was sitting in a ring of guinea-pigs while Ming romped with them, excited as a child at a party. Once their first shyness wore off, the guinea-pigs seemed as tame as the hamsters at school. And yet they were living here, quite wild . . . how queer it was!

But, all in a moment, the party was over.

Someone called from the upper garden. Anna heard her own name, and started up in terror. The guinea-pigs vanished. She listened, and heard Linnet's voice:

"Anna! Anna, where are you? It's dinner-time!"

Then Robin, saying impatiently, "Oh heck. Where's she got to?"

They mustn't come looking for her down here! She raced up the garden. Ming galloped ahead, as though he understood the danger. Whatever happened – even if it meant staying away for good – Robin and Linnet must never find out about the guinea-pigs.

10

It did seem, that afternoon, as though the wilderness were lost for ever. Or, at least, until Mother was out of hospital, and they were home. Then, she would find her way there again by the back lane. But how long would that be? She wanted to go there now, at once, not to waste a minute of this surprising day.

At dinner she asked Mrs Pringle,

"When do you think they'll let Mother out?"

As a rule Mrs Pringle was very good about giving straight answers; but now she only smiled and said,

"I'm going to visit her this afternoon. I'll take the car. There *might* be some good news."

"Yes, but when – ?"

"I think we'd better wait and see what they say."

Linnet had been watching her thoughtfully. Now she asked abruptly,

"What were you doing, Anna, down the garden?"

Taken by surprise, she lost all her new poise, and blushed and mumbled.

"Nothing. Looking for blackberries . . ."

"Oh," said Mrs Pringle, "did you find any? You might all go and pick some for supper."

Anna almost choked. But Robin said in disgust,

"Oh Mum, no. How *boring*." And Linnet,

"It's an awful place. All nettly and beastly."

"Yes. Beastly," Anna said quickly. Well, that was true. Squirrel, mouse, magpie, spiders, guinea-pigs.

"Anyway," Linnet added, "there won't be time."

They were to spend the afternoon at a cinema at the end of the road. An older girl was going with them, a teenager from the next-door flat. Anna guessed that, after yesterday, Mrs Pringle was wary about leaving the three of them alone together . . . and what a nuisance *that* was! With Cheryl there to boss them, she'd never get a chance to slip away in the dark.

She sat glumly through the first film, hardly bothering to watch. In the interval, Robin and Linnet went to queue for ices. Anna stayed where she was, shaking her head when Cheryl offered to pay. Linnet, sliding past, said spitefully,

"Poor old Anastasia. She'd *much* rather go and pick blackberries."

Cheryl seemed to know all about the twins. She gave Anna a fruit gum and asked,

"What did Smarty mean by that?"

She sounded like an ally. And Anna suddenly burst out,

"Oh look – I *would* rather, really. Pick blackberries, I mean, down the garden. Mrs Pringle said she'd like some . . . you don't mind, do you?"

"But you'll miss half the programme!"

"But it's *boring*," she cried, imitating Robin. "And – and my cat's all alone, and – won't you give me the key, please? Then I can take him too – "

"You and your cat!" Cheryl hesitated. "Well – don't get run over, O.K.? Or they'll say it's my fault . . ."

"Oh, honestly . . . Of course I won't, I go shopping for my mother, often and often – quick, before they come back! Oh *thanks* Cheryl . . ."

Anna sat under the fence, resting in the shade, waiting for the guinea-pigs.

She thought they must be dozing in the brilliant heat; but she didn't mind. It was lovely here. She sighed happily, thinking of Robin and Linnet, shut away safely till tea-time watching *Swallows and Amazons*. This was better than Wild Cat Island. She might name it Wild Guinea-pig

Island – and it had a wild cat as well. Ming had slipped away to join his new friends.

It hadn't taken her long to fill a jug with blackberries, and stow it away in the cool shady cave. As she was picking them a red butterfly perched on the brambles, flirting its wings in the sun. Ming gazed at it with interest. Then a huge wasp zoomed overhead, and another, and Anna stopped picking to stare after them. They were dark yellow, three times as big as any wasp she'd ever seen. They must be HORNETS.

Ming was startled too: his eyes rolled, following their flight in alarm. When a third appeared, hovering around, he crouched and eyed it with distrust. Then he ran under the brambles and stayed there out of sight.

Beside her, as she leaned against the fence, she saw a large web with several dead flies. The spider was climbing out of the web, moving slowly, as though it had had a tiring day and meant to take a nap. It crept into a niche in the fence, and curled up beside a withered blackberry that had lodged there: and then Anna found herself blinking in amazement. The spider no longer looked fat and juicy. It seemed to have turned itself into another old dried-up blackberry – you couldn't tell which was which. No hungry bird would have looked twice at either of them.

This was the drowsiest hour of the day. A large bumble-bee clung to a bushy plant with flowers like small white snapdragons. Anna touched its glossy black fur with a careful finger, and it only buzzed and waved its front legs lazily.

The nettle patch close by was baking in the heat. She saw ladybirds under the leaves, and leant nearer to look at them. Then she drew back sharply, and whispered *"Oh . . ."*

Something floated up from the nettles, hung for a moment in the air, drifted, and slowly faded. A smoke-ring. As though some tiny creature – a mouse with a grass-seed cigarette? a leprechaun? a caterpillar with a hookah, like the one in *Alice in Wonderland*? – were sitting down there puffing away. If she'd been younger she might have looked for something of the sort. As it was, she felt she must be dreaming. Because here was another, and there too – tiny perfect smoke-rings. They couldn't be anything else?

She picked up a twig and stirred the nettles. More rings drifted clear. And then she laughed.

Of course! She saw what was happening. Nettle flowers, toasting in the sun, were sending out little puffs of yellowish dust that twirled into eddying rings as it floated. A pity, in a way, that she'd found the answer . . .

And then a frightening thing happened.

Intent on this mystery, she'd forgotten to keep watch. All at once there were steps, quite near, and low voices. A boy and girl came round the brambles, and stood with their backs to her, looking down into the undergrowth where the guinea-pigs were hiding.

Robin and Linnet. They'd tracked her here, after all.

11

The sick terror and panic lasted only a moment. Anna had started up; and when they turned round, she saw it wasn't the twins. But they weren't strangers either. They were Emily and Jody, who had helped to rescue Ming from that tree in the park.

Anna and Emily spoke together: "What are you doing here?"

There was a pause, and they eyed each other doubtfully. It was Anna who answered.

"I've been staying here. With the Pringles."

When she said that name, she saw their faces change. Doubt changed to fear and dismay. Emily said slowly, "The Pringles – !" Jody said, "Oh *no*." They looked at one another in a hunted sort of way.

In a flash Anna realized – They know about the guinea-pigs too! But they don't know if I do. And they're scared in case Robin and Linnet . . . She cried at once,

"It's all right. They don't come here. And they

don't know about –" then she stopped, thinking, Perhaps these two don't either? Perhaps I'm the first to find them. Shall I keep it a secret?

Emily said in a frozen voice,

"Go on. Don't know about *what*?"

There was a long silence. Anna pulled a grass stalk to shreds: she was struggling to make up her mind. They'd helped her before – surely she could trust them?

Suddenly she pointed to the brambles. From every tunnel and pathway in the undergrowth, a small white head was poking. All but one: the face that peered from that was also white, but it had black patches and wild green eyes. Ming.

Emily and Jody looked from the guinea-pigs to the intruder, and from him to Anna; and they all grinned.

Ming bounded out and galloped round in a circle, with a rippling mew of greeting. Then he stopped short and stared at Emily and Jody, and a puzzled look came into his eyes: a thinking look, Anna felt. As though he were trying to recall something he used to do, long ago, when he met new people. Then it came back to him. He ran up to them, rubbed round their legs and rolled over on his back, wriggling and laughing up at them.

Watching him, Anna felt huge relief and happiness: *I never thought he'd do that again.* The other two were squatting down, laughing and stroking him. Then Emily said,

"Come on. We've got to feed the piglets."

Anna saw that they were carrying bulging paper bags. They began to whistle softly, and the guinea-pigs ran out, as though at a well-known signal. Jody shifted a loose plank in the fence and climbed through into the next-door garden. The flock trooped after him like sheep through a hurdle. Mini-sheep. Ming bounded after them like a frivolous sheepdog. Anna squeezed through, and then Emily, and the plank was put back.

Anna gazed around. They were in another wilderness, not quite like the one they'd left, but a far cry from Mr Mali's trim garden. Blackberries and nettles grew here too; but also there were roses, and bushes with scarlet berries, and clumps of bushy flowers, Michaelmas daisies and golden rod, thick with bees. The grass had been cut, but the cutter had left patches of daisies, white clover and other flowers. There was a conker tree, and an almond, and a sweet chestnut, all covered with yellowing nuts. That squirrel would be busy for weeks.

The guinea-pigs ran over to a thick shrubbery and then stopped outside, waiting. The food bags were emptied on the grass: lettuce leaves, carrots, apple peel, crusts. The guinea-pigs feasted. Ming settled down with them, chewing daintily at a crust; and Anna laughed.

"He won't *ever* touch bread," she explained.

73

Emily and Jody sprawled on the turf, looking quite at home: and a swarm of questions danced on the tip of Anna's tongue. She couldn't keep them in any longer.

"How did *you* find the guinea-pigs? And – do the people let you come here? Or don't they know either? Suppose they find us in their garden?"

They stared at her in surprise. Then Emily said gently,

"I thought you knew. We live here. It's our garden."

"And," Jody added, "they're ours too."

74

Anna was dumbfounded. At last she said,

"I *didn't* know. You see . . . I thought they were wild."

"So they are, sort of."

Her look of wistful envy set them off. A whole saga came pouring out.

"Dad bought them for us, when we came here last year – "

"And they got out of the hutch – "

"We couldn't find them anywhere, we thought a dog – "

"And then we heard them in the bushes – there were just two then – "

"Yes, and we never thought they'd live through the winter – "

"We used to leave food for them, they wouldn't come out till we'd gone, they didn't know us then, you see – "

"And we put drain-pipes for them to hide in – "

"And when the snow melted, there they were! And they had babies, and got quite tame – "

"Yes, and then they had another lot, and they got through the fence and started living over there too – "

"Doesn't matter you see, those people don't use their garden – "

"We bring them back to feed, every day – "

Anna sighed. "Oh, you're so lucky."

"Well – " Emily glanced at her brother, and asked,

"Would you like one? Or a pair? We've got such a pack of them – "

"Oh *yes* . . ." Anna said eagerly.

But then she had a vision: Mr Mali's precious flower-beds, overrun with squeaking burrowing guinea-pigs. One hedgehog, one bewitching feather-footed cat, yes – but that was as far as he should be asked to go. You couldn't expect another miracle.

Her face fell, and she murmured,

"No, I can't. You see, we haven't any garden, not of our own."

"You can share them here, then."

"Could I? Can I really?" Her face alight again, she cried,

"I'll help you feed them – I can bring carrots and everything, it's not far to come, just over the old railway – along that lane – "

"Yes," Jody nodded. "Where the foxes are."

"*What?*"

"Didn't you know? They live in the railway banks."

"You can hear them bark, nights, in the winter – "

"And they come and raid our dustbins – "

"But they can't eat the piglets, they're quite safe in those drain-pipes."

Emily added, "And Dad says, next summer, if we get up early enough, he'll take us to see the cubs."

"Cubs!"

"Yes, they come out and play on the banks, when no one's about. Come with us, why don't you?"

The sun dipped behind the trees. Long shadows crept over the grass as they talked. Then it was time to go.

"School next week," said Emily. "See you then?"

School . . . she realized that she wasn't dreading it any more. Next term was going to be fun – and coming here after school – and looking for foxes –

"Yes," Anna nodded. "See you then."

She put Ming over the fence, scrambled through and turned to wave. She was in such a daze, with all that had happened, and all that was going to happen, that it was some time before she realized what she was hearing. People in the upper garden, talking – and now they were calling her.

"Anna! Come and see who's here!"

Mrs Pringle . . . she remembered the jug of blackberries, hidden in the cave, and scooped it out, and started up the slope. But a moment later she stopped dead, holding her breath to listen. Those others – up there, talking to the Pringles – they sounded like – *could* they be – ?

"*A*-nna. *A*-nna!"

Mother's call. Yes, it *was*. She was *here* . . . and then something else: a long trilling bird-like whistle. Only one person whistled like that. Daddy . . . he was here too. They'd all be going home at last.

And now, as she ran, Anna was smiling to herself. Partly because of Mother and Daddy; but also for another reason. Because of something she'd overheard from Emily and Jody.

As they marched up their own garden path, their voices had come back clearly. Jody's first, sharp with anxiety:

"Look. Are you sure she won't tell *them*?"

Then Emily's, saying calmly,

"Of course I'm sure. Anna's not like them. She's nice."

"Y-e-e-e-s. I know." He sounded surprised; but nothing like as surprised as Anna felt. After days of being Little Nasty, she could hardly believe they'd said that. But it was true. Jody spoke again.

"I quite like her, I think. Her and that funny cat."

NOTE

Linnet's jigsaw is based on a real
picture, *The Graham Children* by
Hogarth, and you can see it at the
Tate Gallery in London.